The Girl Who Danced with Dolphins

Story by Frank DeSaix ~ Pictures by Debbi Durland DeSaix

Farrar Straus Giroux

New York

Library of Congress catalog card number: 90-27007
Published simultaneously in Canada by HarperCollins*CanadaLtd*
Color separations by Imago Publishing Ltd.
Printed and bound in the United States of America
by Horowitz/Rae Book Manufacturers
Designed by Martha Rago
First edition, 1991

For Jeanne Cummings,
whose kindness made our work possible

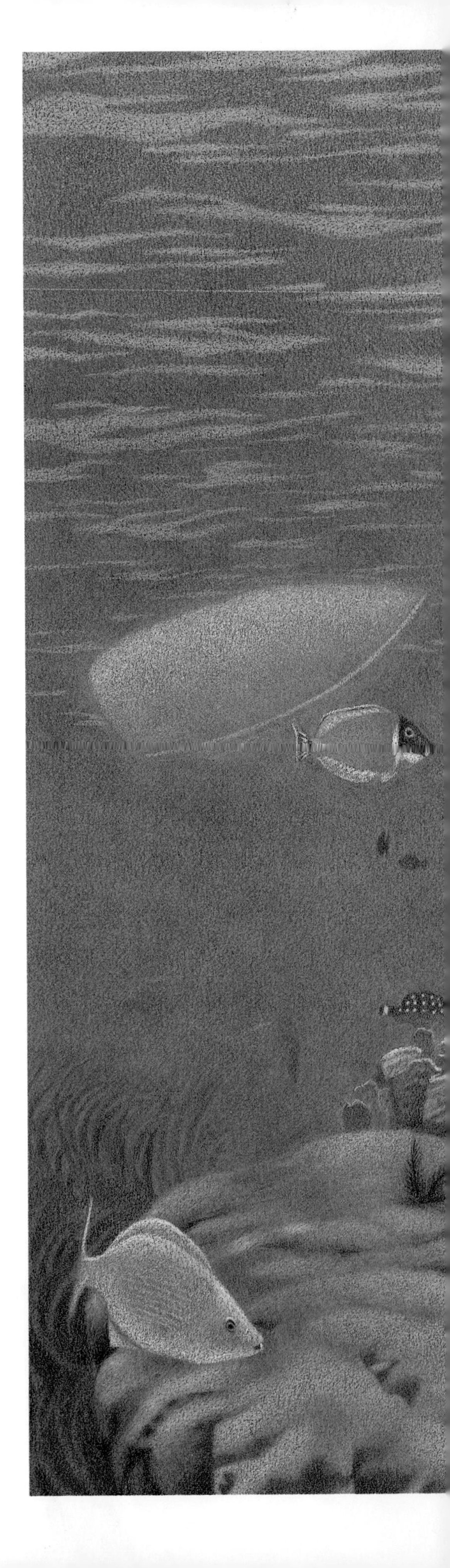

Adrianne floated over mountains of coral. She stretched out her arm, and a butterfly fish nibbled her fingertip. It tickled, and she flinched, and the creature fluttered away, zigzag. Sea grasses fanned softly below her.

Nearby, the belly of Grandpa's dinghy hung like an eggshell. The sea was quiet and comforting, and it stroked every movement she made. A skate flowed past. A bit of sand wriggled, then settled.

Adrianne surfaced and tossed her snorkel to her grandfather.

"I don't need it!" she shouted.

"So, you're a mermaid already?"

"Yes!" She laughed between breaths. "Yes! It's neat!"

Adrianne squinted in the sun-bright air. There was only the sky, easy waves, and Grandpa bobbing with his little boat. She cleared her mask.

"Stay over the reef, Annie. It's safer."

Adrianne nodded, sucked in a deep breath, and dived.

Jewels of life appeared. Shrimp tiptoed over spiny urchins. Anemones waved. A moray's face slunk into a crevice. Oarlocks clattered from the hollow boat.

Adrianne glanced up. Streams of bubbles boiled under Grandpa's dinghy. He was rowing toward her, fast. Between them, a shadow loomed.

At first she wasn't afraid, but stayed very still. Then the shark rippled, like a snake, and slipped sideways, toward her. She tried to back away and felt much too slow.

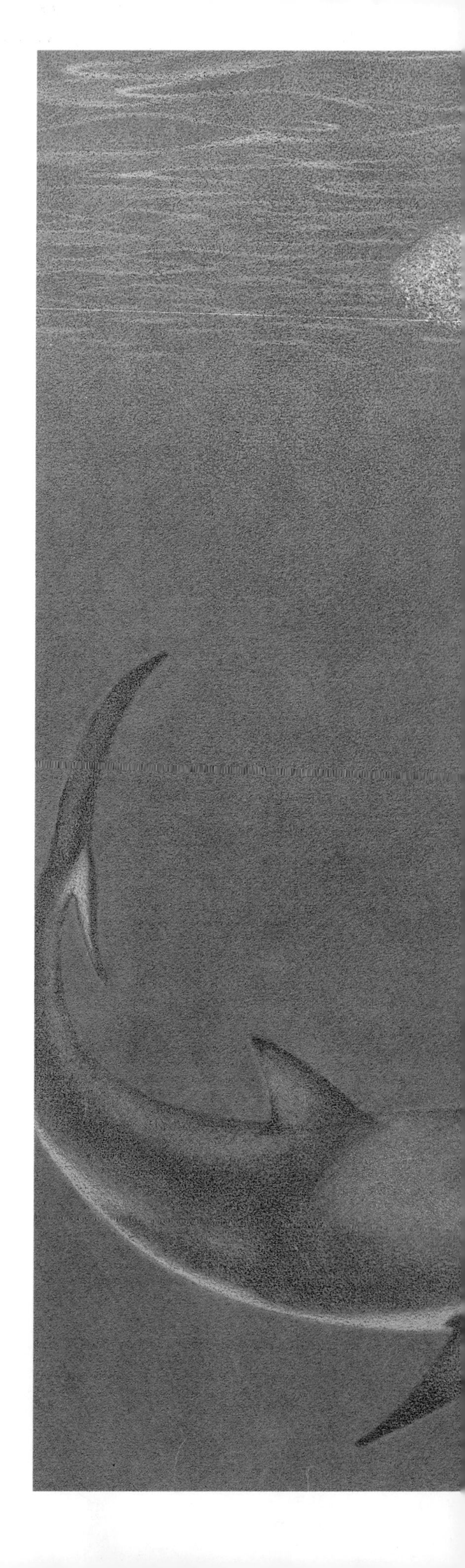

Suddenly, a great, sleek body was right there, in front of her. A dolphin! It shouldered her upward. In a splash of sunlight, her grandfather grasped her arm and swung her into the boat.

"Shark!" Adrianne coughed.

"I know."

"A dolphin saved me."

"I know."

Adrianne looked into the ocean. The reef below shifted lightly with the waves. The shark and the dolphin were gone.

Moonlight whitened Adrianne's room. Her grandfather sat on her bed. He held both her hands in one of his.

"I was scared, Grandpa."

"Me, too." He spoke softly.

"Why did the dolphin save me?"

"He heard your heart, Annie."

"I wish I could thank him," she whispered.

Grandpa touched her hair, smiled, then drew the mosquito net closed. Adrianne snuggled into the great, warm dent that he had left in the bed.

From her window a path of moonlight glistened over the sea. The dolphins were out there. She closed her eyes and tried to imagine. If she were a dolphin, she would swim, oh, how she would swim. She would soar through the sea the way swallows fly. She would burst from the sea and pirouette for the moon.

She arched over and entered the water in a silver blanket of bubbles.

Familiar chirps greeted her. She was a dolphin. And the sea that seemed so dark to humans was bright and clear for dolphins, bright with sounds. Things bumped and moaned and clattered and clicked, and twinkled in her mind. A herd of whales roamed a nearby valley, and their song rose like a sunrise.

The dolphins surfaced for air, then descended together in a graceful arc. Through clouds of mackerel and past forests of kelp, the herd of dolphins led Adrianne downward. One nudged her playfully, and she nudged him right back. Far ahead, something glittered.

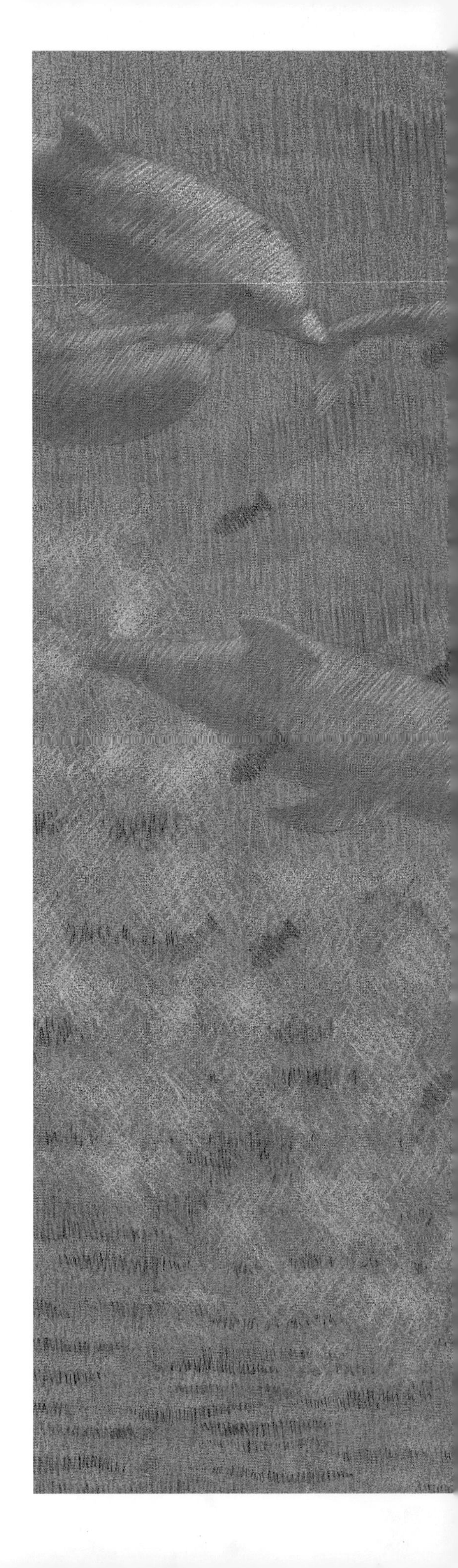

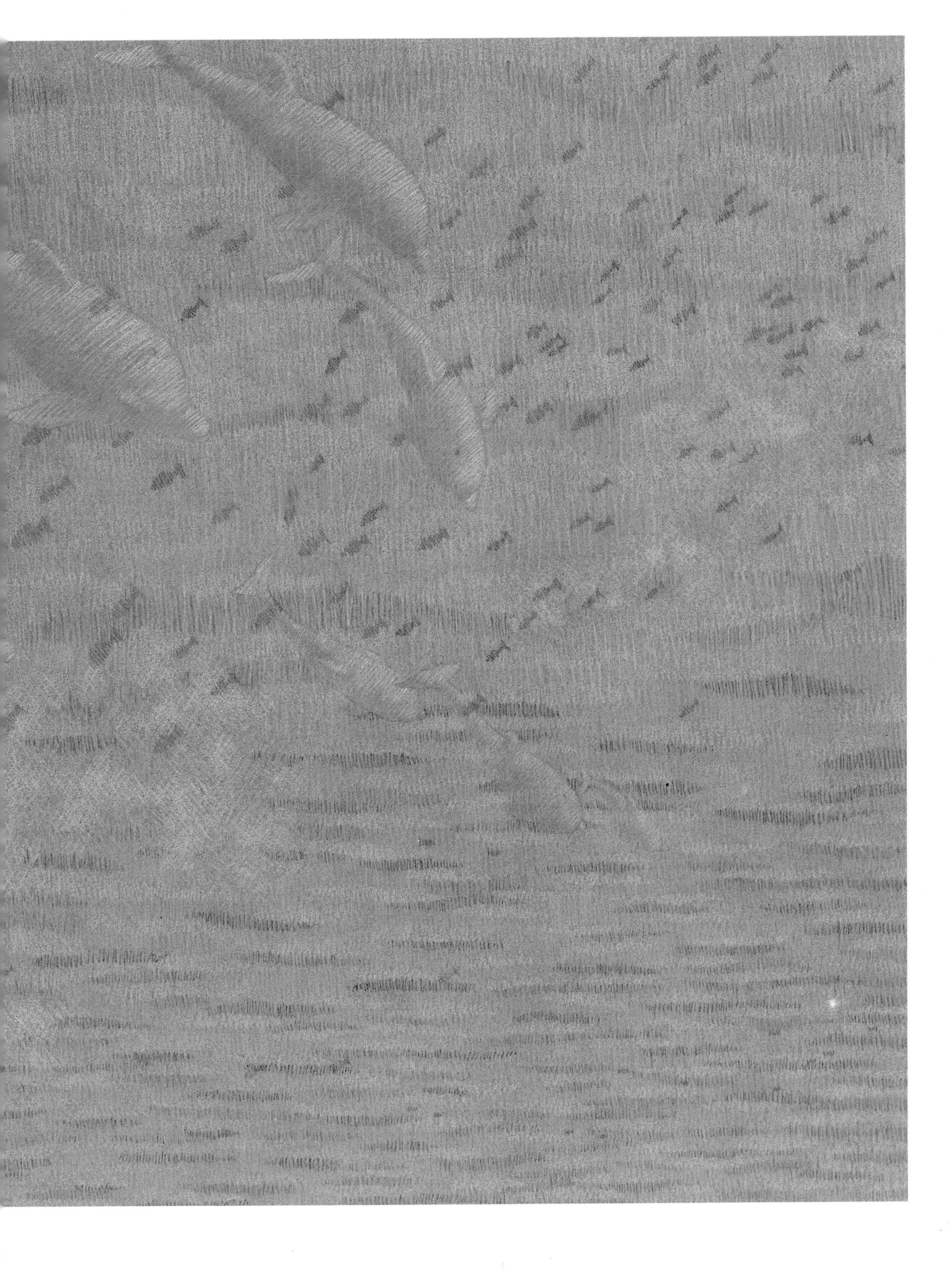

The tiny jewel grew and grew into a brilliant shell. It was gliding up from the deepest of depths. Adrianne nosed close and caught the fragrance of a nautilus, as rare as an orchid.

All around her, Adrianne heard the dancing heartbeats of the others. They circled the curious shell. Bathed in the limelight of their calls, the nautilus gleamed as brightly as a pearl in moonlight, and swam serenely on.

Adrianne turned skyward. The others swept past her. The flight of dolphins rose in a dance. They tumbled and touched like children, and Adrianne followed their wake.

Adrianne swam faster and passed them, then faster still, with all her strength. She flashed through layers of purple and blue, and she burst from the sea into starlight, and stretched, and soared, and turned a pirouette for the moon.

Adrianne opened her eyes. The moonlight was gone, and the darkness was tinged with sunrise. She dressed hurriedly.

There were smells of oatmeal and coffee brewing. Grandpa sat in his rocker on the porch. As she passed him, he spoke quietly. "Go quickly, Annie."

She ran to the beach. There was nothing there. The breakers sparkled in the morning air. Adrianne waited.

Two waves cradled a glistening piece of moonlight. Seafoam carried the empty shell to her feet. In the dawn, it glowed.

Adrianne knelt and carefully picked up the worn and ancient shell of a nautilus. Then she stood. Beyond the breakers, a single dolphin arched away from her and out to sea. Very softly, Adrianne whispered, "Thank you."